Praise for the
Urgency Emergency!
series

★"Top-notch medical care in an equally terrific early reader that will appeal to preschoolers, new readers of all ages, and anyone else who appreciates droll humor and an inventive plot."
—*Kirkus Reviews* starred review

★"New readers are in for a treat with these British imports."
—*Horn Book* starred review

"Archer's thickly painted illustrations exude personality and humor, and emerging readers will get a kick out of seeing the repercussions of a familiar story play out in an emergency room setting."
—*Publishers Weekly*

"There is plenty of sly humor in the text."—*School Library Journal*

"The folkloric connections broaden the use possibilities for libraries and classrooms, and the titles could inspire student writing or dramatic projects in a similar vein, while the medical situations are surprisingly educational."
—*Bulletin of the Center for Children's Books*, recommended

"Valuable lessons about overcoming fears and setting aside differences for others are emphasized."
—*Library Media Connection*

To the wonderful, inspirational Matthew

Library of Congress Cataloging-in-Publication
data is on file with the publisher.

Text and illustrations copyright © 2015 by Dosh Archer
Published in 2015 by Albert Whitman & Company
ISBN 978-0-8075-8356-2

Printed in China
10 9 8 7 6 5 4 3 2 1 NP 20 19 18 17 16 15

For more information about Albert Whitman & Company,
visit our web site at www.albertwhitman.com.

URGENCY EMERGENCY!

Humpty's Fall

Dosh Archer

Albert Whitman & Company
Chicago, Illinois

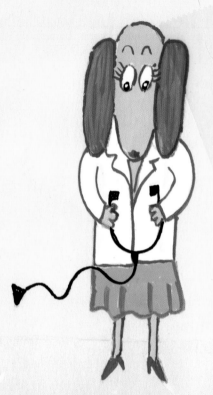

It was another busy day at City Hospital. Doctor Glenda was checking her stethoscope and Nurse Percy was cleaning up Weasel, who was covered in bubblegum.

He had blown a great big bubble
and it had burst. Little pink bits of
it were sticking to his fur.

Just then
the ambulance
arrived.

"Urgency Emergency!" cried the Pengamedics. "We have a cracked egg coming through!" Two of the king's men had come along. They were the ones who had called the ambulance.

"Let me examine him," said
Doctor Glenda.

"It is just as I thought. His head is cracked and the yolk is spilling out."

"Can you tell us your name and what happened?" asked Doctor Glenda.

"We saw it all," said one of the king's men. "It was Weasel. He always blows big bubbles with his bubblegum until they pop. This time he blew a huge bubble right behind Humpty.

It made a really loud
POP! No wonder
Humpty fell over."

"His head is quite damaged," said Doctor Glenda, "and it has been made worse because someone moved him before the ambulance arrived."

"We were only trying to put him together again," said one of the king's men.

"He is losing too much yolk.
We must act quickly. There is
not a moment to spare," said
Doctor Glenda.

"But what can we do?" cried
Nurse Percy. "You cannot stitch
him back together. You will
never get a needle through his
hard shell."

Doctor Glenda looked around.
"I have thought of a plan. Bring
Weasel here!"

Weasel came and stood next to Doctor Glenda. "I'm sorry," he said. "I didn't mean to scare Humpty. I didn't know he would fall."

"Weasel," said Doctor Glenda,
"give me your headphones and
spit out the bubblegum."

"But these are my best
headphones," said Weasel,
"and this is my last piece
of bubblegum."

"I don't feel well…" said Humpty.
"My yolk is draining away."

"Do you want to make it up to Humpty or not?" asked Doctor Glenda.

"Yes," said Weasel, and he handed over the headphones and bubblegum.

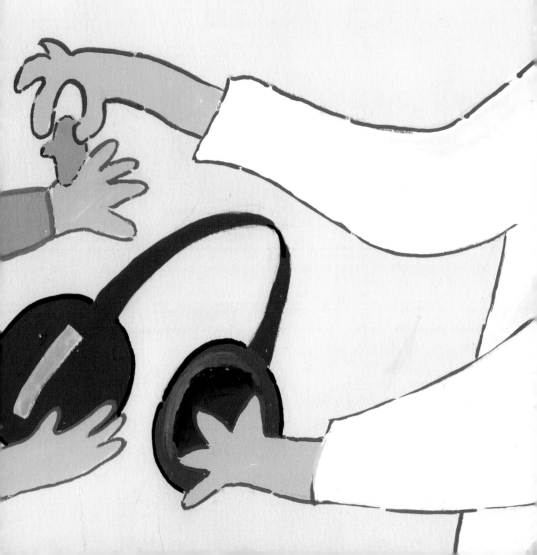

Doctor Glenda placed the headphones very carefully over Humpty's head, taking great care not to touch the crack.

Then she tightened them up as far as they would go so that they squeezed the crack together.

Doctor Glenda pressed the sticky,
squashy bubblegum along the
crack in the shell.

"The headphones will hold
the crack together, and the gum
will stop it from coming apart,"
Nurse Percy told Humpty.

"How long will I have to stay in
the hospital?" asked Humpty.
"Three days," said Doctor Glenda.
"That is a long time," said Humpty.

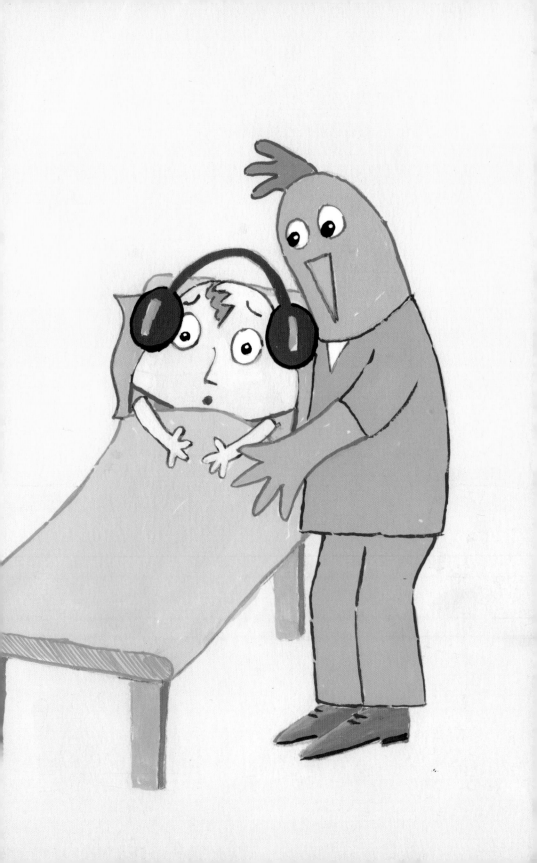

"Don't worry," said Weasel. "You can borrow my music player to listen to through the headphones. I've got lots of great songs."

"Thank you," said Humpty.

"Let's get you cleaned up," said
Nurse Percy. He used a special
cleaning liquid to get the rest of
the bubblegum off Weasel's fur.

Weasel said thank you very
nicely and went home.

Before the king's men left, Doctor Glenda had a talk with them. "Only move an injured person if they are in a dangerous place.

If they are in a safe situation,
keep them still until the
ambulance arrives."

"OK," said the king's men and got on their horses and went back to the parade.

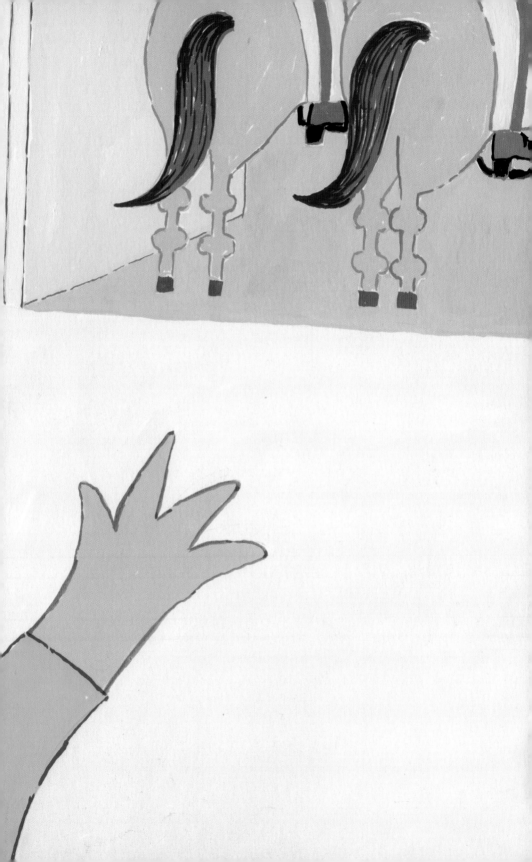

"I can never thank you enough," said Humpty.

"All in a day's work," said Doctor Glenda. "All in a day's work."

It had been a very sticky situation, but thanks to Nurse Percy's care and Doctor Glenda's quick thinking, Humpty would soon be better.

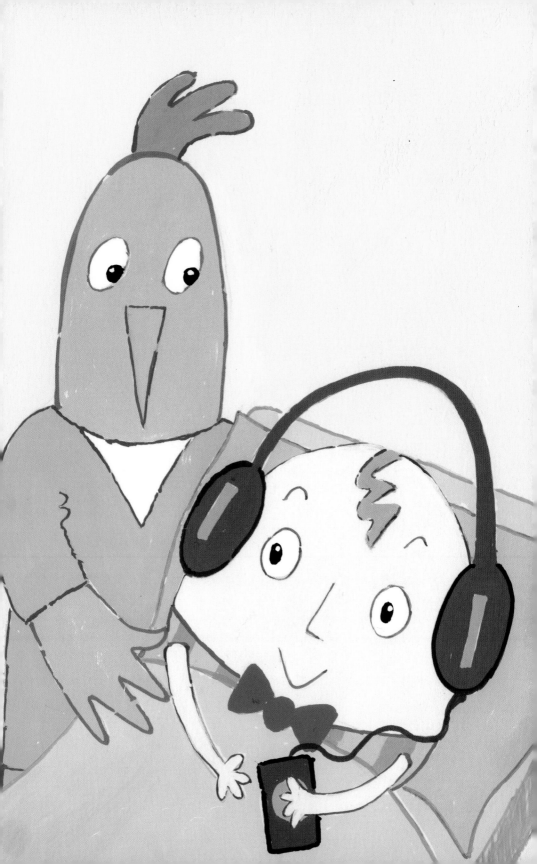